THE MYSTERY

AT

Mount Vernon

Home of America's First President, George Washington

Managing Editor: Sherry Moss
Assistant Editor: Susan Walworth
Cover Photo Courtesy of the Mount Vernon Ladies' Association
Cover Design: Vicki DeJoy
Content Design: Randolyn Friedlander

Gallopade International is introducing SAT words that kids need to know in each new book that we publish. The SAT words are bold in the story. Look for this special logo beside each word in the glossary. Happy Learning!

Gallopade is proud to be a member and supporter of these educational organizations and associations:

American Booksellers Association
American Library Association
International Reading Association
National Association for Gifted Children
The National School Supply and Equipment Association
The National Council for the Social Studies
Museum Store Association
Association of Partners for Public Lands
Association of Booksellers for Children
Association for the Study of African American Life and History
National Alliance of Black School Educators

Once upon a time...

Hmm, kids keep asking me to write a mystery book. What shall I do?

Mimi

Write one about spiders!

Papa said...

Why don't you set the stories in real locations?

That's a great idea! And if I do that, I might as well choose real kids as characters in the stories! But which kids would I pick?

MiMi, PiCK ME, PiCK ME!

ME, TOO, MiMi, PiCK ME, TOO!

Christina

Grant

Pick me!

You two really are characters, that's all I've got to say!

Yes you are! And, of course I choose you! But what should I write about?

National Parks!

SCARY PLACES!

Famous Places!

FUN PLACES!

Disney World!

New York City!

Dracula's Castle

GRAND CANYON

On the *Mystery Girl* airplane ...

I CAN FLY US anyWHERE!

Or aboard
the *Mimi!*

Take me to the
Forbidden City!

Or by surfboard,
rickshaw,
motorbike,
camel ...

All great ideas!
I can put a lot of history,

MYSTERY,

legend, lore, and laughs in
the books! We can use other boys and girls
in the books. It will be educational and fun!

Good
stuff!

The *Mystery Girl* is all revved up—let's go!

You mean now?

LET'S GO!

Mystery Girl

And so, Mimi, Papa, Christina, and Grant took off aboard the *Mystery Girl* and America's National Mystery Book Series—where the adventure is real and so are the characters! —was born.

START YOUR ADVENTURE TODAY!

READ THE BOOK!

GO ONLINE!

Yikes! That was close!

TRACK YOUR ADVENTURES!

APPLY TO BE A CHARACTER!

Rats!

1
CHOP PHOOEY

Christina felt tense for no good reason. It was springtime in Washington. The cherry trees throughout the city, a gift from Japan many years ago, were covered with blooms that reminded her of thousands of tiny, pink butterflies. The sun was shining, and birds were singing like rock stars. Still, something wasn't quite right.

Christina and her brother Grant had been to the nation's capital many times with their grandparents Mimi and Papa. Each time, her dream of visiting Mount Vernon, home of America's first president and Revolutionary War hero, George Washington, had never happened. But this time, Mimi had promised. Papa pushed his cowboy hat back on his head, leaned against a cherry tree, and sighed. "When that woman finds a library, she loses all track of time," he grumbled.

Mimi, a mystery writer, had spent most of the week at the Library of Congress. She was researching a new mystery—one so mysterious she wouldn't even tell them what it was to be about. Christina had a sneaky suspicion it had something to do with the Revolutionary War.

Papa glanced impatiently at his watch. "Sure hope she didn't get lost," he said.

Grant had gone into a nearby toy shop to kill time while Christina and Papa waited for almost an hour outside a bike rental shop near Washington. It wasn't their usual way of getting around, but what better way to get to Mount Vernon and at the same time enjoy the area's most beautiful season?

Christina had just noticed black clouds on the distant horizon when a sudden whirlwind scooped cherry blossoms off the sidewalk and sent them in a pink blizzard straight toward her. Blinded, she froze as something grabbed at her shoulders.

Christina blinked hard but saw nothing but a fuzzy, gray blur passing her face. Was a rascally raccoon playing pranks on her? Another hard blink revealed a glint of silver from a hatchet blade. Raccoons don't carry hatchets, Christina thought in panic. Is there a madman on the loose?

"Papa!" Christina screamed, stumbling to the spot where she had last seen her grandfather.

Papa caught Christina just as she tripped. "Whoa there, little darlin," he said in his deep, charming cowboy voice. "You know I love to dance with ya, but is the sidewalk the best place?"

"Someone's after me," Christina stammered and grabbed Papa around the waist. "And he's got a hatchet."

Christina felt Papa's belly jiggling with laughter.

"I think you better look again," he said between good-natured guffaws.

Christina rubbed her eyes. The fuzzy, gray image came into focus. It was only Grant!

"Looks like your brother has found some nifty souvenirs," Papa said with another laugh.

Grant struck a pose with the hatchet. What Christina had thought was a raccoon was a gray wig like old men wore in the 1700s.

"Guess who?" Grant said.

"A little old lady having a bad hair day?" Christina suggested.

Grant frowned. "If you knew anything about history, you'd know I'm George Washington," he said.

"You may think you're George," Christina replied. "But I cannot tell a lie. You've got that wig on backwards. The ponytail is supposed to be in the back, not coming out of your forehead."

Grant eyed the blossoms that had landed on Christina's shoulders. "Well, you should really do something about your bad case of pink dandruff," he said.

"Ha, ha, ha," Christina replied, rolling her eyes and brushing the blossoms from her shoulders.

"Here goes!" Grant shouted, raising the hatchet into position to give the nearest cherry tree a chop.

"Grant!" Mimi yelled. "Stop!" She scurried toward them, her red high heels wobbling on the cobblestone sidewalk. "Don't you dare hit that tree!"

Grant shot her a **mischievous** grin. "No worries, Mimi," he said. "It's only plastic."

"You need to do some more research on that cherry tree tale," Mimi said. "Most historians believe the famous story of a young George Washington chopping down his father's favorite cherry tree and then telling him the truth never really happened."

"You're kidding!" Grant said with a disappointed look.

"That's right," Mimi confirmed. "A preacher named Mason Weems used that story to teach boys like you not to lie."

"Guess that means I can never tell Christina how beautiful she is again," Grant said with another mischievous grin.

"If we don't mosey down that trail," Papa said, "those black clouds are going to rain on our parade."

Mimi changed from her red heels into her red tennis shoes. Of course, Papa had also rented a bike in her favorite color. As they buckled their helmets, the bike shop owner stepped outside to see them off. An old man with cloudy blue eyes, he gave them a warning that Christina thought was as **ominous** as the clouds.

"I'd be careful if I were you," he said. "There have been some strange things happening at that old mansion."

2
WAYWARD WIG

"Beat you to the top!" Grant hollered. He wheeled his lime green bike past Christina and pedaled hard. The gray ponytail of his wig wiggled furiously under his helmet.

"Don't forget, it's not called Mount Vernon for nothing!" Christina yelled after him. While waiting for Mimi, Christina had studied the trail map. She knew this final climb would be the worst, so she paced herself. She wasn't planning to let Grant win. She knew the best way to beat him would be to let his blast of speed wear him out long before he reached the top.

Christina waved to Mimi and Papa, lagging like Sunday drivers far behind, and stood up on the pedals of her blue bike. The springtime air was unusually humid and heavy for April, and it made Christina's shoulder-length, brown hair bushier than Grant's wig. At least I'm not likely to run into any of my friends, she thought.

Grant had almost reached the crest of the hill when he stopped and planted his feet on the pavement. Christina smiled with satisfaction. She knew her brother would run out of steam before he won the race.

"What's the matter?" Christina crowed as she flew past. "Run out of gas?"

Grant didn't reply. Christina pumped the pedals and gasped when she reached the crest. Standing stately beyond a sea of freshly mown grass was perhaps the United States' most historic home—Mount Vernon. The simple, white mansion with its red roof practically glowed in front of the dark clouds that still threatened their visit.

"Can you believe that George Washington actually slept here?" Christina asked her brother. He gave no answer. "Grant?"

Her brother had plenty of time to catch up by now. Christina looked in her bike mirror. She could see Grant's bike on the trail edge, but he was nowhere to be seen!

Christina knew Grant could never pass up an opportunity to use the bathroom outdoors. He had probably slipped behind a bush to do just that. But the bike shop owner's warning still swirled in her head. Christina turned around and aimed her bike back down the hill. "Grant!" she called. "Where are you?"

Naked branches just sprouting green buds clawed at Christina's clothes while she pushed through the brush beside the trail. "You better not be hiding!" Christina warned. She braced herself, waiting for Grant to jump out and say, "Boo!" Nothing happened.

"You can't scare me, I know you're here somewhere!" Christina yelled. She took more careful steps but stopped with a squeal. Something furry was tickling her toe. "OOOOOH!" she yelped, expecting to see a wild animal about to bite her foot. What she saw frightened her even more. It was Grant's gray wig.

3
A CLUE TO CHEW

Christina spied a boy and girl who looked like they'd walked right out of George Washington's era. The boy wore brown knee breeches and shoes with silver buckles, and the girl wore a billowy, pink dress that almost reached the ground.

"Can you help me?" Christina asked frantically. "My brother's missing!"

"Follow us!" the boy commanded. "There's a security guard at the Texas gate!"

Christina was explaining her brother's disappearance to the guard when she heard Papa ask, "What's the ruckus?" She whirled to see her grandparents holding their bikes, and bringing up the rear was Grant. He looked like a hurricane had combed his blonde curls, and there were tiny scratches on his arms, but he was A-OK.

"Never mind," Christina said sheepishly to the security guard.

"Thanks for finding my wig," Grant said when he noticed Christina holding it like a dead animal in her hand.

Christina turned to the boy and girl who had led her to the gate. "Thanks, anyway," she said. "Looks like my brother's been found."

"No problem," the boy said. "We do everything we can to help guests enjoy their visit to Mount Vernon."

"Do you get paid to work here?" Grant asked.

"I wish," the girl answered. "Our mother's the estate historian. Anytime we don't have to be at school, we dress up in period clothes and hang out here. Our mother says there's no better way for us to learn about American history."

"I'm Patrick and this is my sister, Eleanor," the boy said.

"Please call me by my nickname, Nellie," the girl said quickly.

Christina introduced herself and Grant.

"I knew I recognized you!" Patrick said excitedly. "You're the kids who solve mysteries, and that must be Mimi! We've read all your books."

"Glad you like the books," Christina said. "But we're at Mount Vernon for fun and to learn about George Washington. We don't want to get mixed up in any mysteries."

"The best place to start learning is at the Ford Orientation Center and the Donald W. Reynolds Museum and Education Center," Nellie suggested. "Then you know more about what you're looking at. Patrick and I can give you a personal tour."

"Would you?" Christina asked excitedly. "What are we waiting for?" Mimi asked. "Those clouds are getting closer."

Life-size statues of George and Martha Washington and two small children greeted them inside the Orientation Center.

"Who are these children?" Christina asked. "I didn't think George Washington had any children."

"Don't you know he was called the father of our country?" Grant said in a know-it-all voice.

"You're both right," Patrick explained. "He was called the father of our country simply because without him, our country might never have existed. He led our country to independence by being the commander of the Continental Army during the Revolutionary War. He never had any children of his own, but his wife, Martha, had two young children when the Washingtons married. John Parke and Martha Parke Custis became his stepchildren."

Christina wanted to read about every artifact on display in the museum. Grant couldn't wait to see Washington's chompers.

Studying the teeth in the glass case, Grant asked, "How do you eat with wooden teeth without getting splinters in your tongue?"

"He never had dentures made of wood," Nellie said.

"First, the cherry tree story and now, the wooden teeth," Grant said with a sigh. "Guess nothing I knew about Washington was true. What are these dentures made from?"

"Believe me, it's worse than wood," Patrick said. "These are made from hippopotamus bone, ivory, and believe it or not, human teeth."

"You mean he was chewing with someone else's teeth?" Grant asked with a look of disgust. "GROSS!"

Christina, who was reading the plaque beneath the teeth, said, "It says here that Washington had several sets of teeth during his lifetime."

"Ha!" said Grant, spotting something stuck behind the plaque. "Looks like someone left a toothpick." He carefully pulled it out.

"You shouldn't touch other people's dirty toothpicks," Christina scolded her brother. She pulled a tissue from her pocket for Grant. When he dropped the toothpick into the tissue, something strange happened. The tiny stick unrolled.

"That's no toothpick," Christina said, showing Patrick and Nellie.

Patrick picked it up. "It looks like parchment paper," he said. He opened the tiny scroll and read:

THIS IS NO TEASE.
ON THESE GROUNDS
ARE MORE OF THESE.

4
SHIVERING SOLDIERS

Christina shivered in the freezing darkness and peered sadly at the Revolutionary soldiers in ragged uniforms. Some of them left trails of blood in the snow as they walked on feet blackened by frostbite. "Those poor men," Christina whispered to Grant. "I feel so sorry for them. They look so cold, tired, and hungry."

Grant brushed the falling snow off his legs. "They can't give up," Grant said. "We'll never win the war if they give up."

Christina watched the men's faces change from despair to hope when General George Washington arrived on his big, gray horse. "Yeah!" she clapped before she realized. "Everything will be OK now. We will win the war!"

Bright lights filled the theater, and Christina realized that she, too, had been dusted with snow.

"There you are!" a tall, attractive woman told Patrick and Nellie. "I've been looking all over for you."

Patrick introduced Christina and Grant to their mother, Sarah Tiller.

"How do you like our interactive theater?" she asked. "Did you feel like you were really at Valley Forge when that snow started to fall?"

"I thought I was turning into an ice pop," Christina said with a shiver.

"It makes you appreciate what those American soldiers went through surviving that tough winter to win our independence from England," Mrs. Tiller said.

Mimi and Papa interrupted their conversation. "We better get to the house tour. I've got to be back in Washington before night," said Mimi.

"That's just not enough time to see everything," Christina **whined**.

Patrick and Nellie gave their mother a "PLEASE!" look.

"Grant and Christina are welcome to stay with us for a few days," Mrs. Tiller told Mimi and Papa. "We'd love to have some more young re-enactors on site. I'll make them earn their keep."

"I've already got the Washington wig and hatchet," Grant said proudly.

"Will you make sure they learn a lot of history?" Mimi asked. "I'd love to give them a test when I pick them up."

"I'll guarantee it," Mrs. Tiller said with a wink. "In fact, why don't you let them give you a personal tour of the place when you come back to pick them up!"

"That sounds like a great plan!" Mimi said. Papa nodded his cowboy hat in agreement.

Outside, the black clouds had arrived at Mount Vernon and chased the beautiful spring day away. Everything was now a soggy mess. After hugs and goodbyes with Mimi and Papa, the kids slogged through the grass to the Mount Vernon Inn Restaurant for steaming mugs of Valley Forge soup. Christina almost felt guilty as the soothing, warm soup flowed down her throat. She knew it was much more than the starving soldiers had enjoyed.

Patrick and Nellie seemed glad that the four of them were alone at last. "So what do you think our clue means?" Patrick asked.

"Do you really think there could be another set of George Washington's teeth hidden somewhere at Mount Vernon?" Christina asked. "If there is, it would be worth a fortune."

"Maybe they're in the pantry or in the refrigerator," Grant suggested. "That way his teeth would be close to his snacks. But personally, I'd rather eat soup than chew my food with someone else's teeth."

"There have been a lot of **archaeological** digs at Mount Vernon," Nellie said. "You'd think everything would have been found by now."

Grant made a curious statement. "That's not what the man in the woods said."

5
FRANK OR PRANK?

"What on earth are you talking about, Grant?" Christina asked.

"I met a man in the woods when I got off the bike trail," Grant explained.

"That reminds me," Christina remembered. "Why'd you get off the trail in the first place?"

"I saw some bushes moving," Grant said. "At first I thought it was the wind. But when I stopped and listened, I could hear someone whistling *Yankee Doodle*. When I got off my bike for a closer look, I heard someone ask, 'You headed to Mount Vernon?'"

Christina shook her head in disbelief. "Grant, you know better than to talk to strangers," she scolded. "Especially if you meet them in the woods."

"It was OK," Grant replied. He grinned as he patted his side. "I had my trusty hatchet for protection. Besides, I could tell he worked here. He was dressed like a Valley Forge soldier in a raggedy uniform. He said his name was Frank."

Patrick and Nellie exchanged curious looks as Grant continued his story.

"Frank said Mount Vernon had revealed a lot about the Washingtons," Grant went on, "but there were plenty of mysteries yet to be solved. 'Keep your eyes and ears open,' he told me. 'You never know what you may find.'"

Patrick finally spoke. "That's odd," he said. "We're here a lot, and we've never seen or heard of anyone dressed like that. And I don't know why anyone who works here would be in the woods on the bike trail."

"Yeah, Grant," Christina agreed. "You're making this up, aren't you? You were disappointed about the whole cherry tree story, so you made up a tale of your own."

"But I'm not making it up!" Grant protested. "He was there. Let's go and see if we can find him."

Dong, Dong, Dong, Dong, Dong. The inn clock struck 5 p.m. "I'm afraid that will have to wait till tomorrow," Nellie said. "It's time to meet Mom."

Outside, the grounds of Mount Vernon were silent as a graveyard at midnight. All the tourists had gone, and the gates were locked tight. Now, Christina could really imagine what it was like to live here, back in an era she could hardly imagine. She stared at the historic house in the late afternoon glow that made it look like the crackly, old paintings Christina had seen of the building in textbooks. More majestic than mysterious, she thought. That's when she spied a shadowy figure pace past an upstairs window...

6
GRANT DOODLE DANDY

Christina had dreamed about the shadowy figure in the window but decided not to tell the others about what she had seen. With a mysterious clue and a stranger in the woods to worry about, she didn't need to add anything else to their worries. Besides, there was always a chance it had just been her imagination.

"Now, don't you look like a dandy," Christina teased her brother when he walked out in his late 18th-century attire complete with a white, ruffly-sleeved shirt, gray knee breeches, stockings, and, of course, his gray wig.

"Dandy?" Grant asked. "I don't even know what that is. I was going for retired, heroic general."

"A dandy is someone dressed in fancy clothes," Christina explained. "You know, like Yankee Doodle Dandy."

Christina had chosen a blue dress with tiny ribbons decorating the puff sleeves from the closet of costumes at Nellie and Patrick's. "Good thing we're about the same size as our new friends," Christina said.

"Yeah," Grant agreed. "When we agreed to spend a few days at Mount Vernon, we forgot the only clothes we had were the ones on our back. We didn't even have any extra underwear, or skivvies, as Papa calls them. It feels kinda weird borrowing Patrick's."

"EWWW!" Christina cried. "Why are you doing that? I'm wearing my own."

"EWWW!" Grant cried. "You're wearing dirty underwear?"

"Of course not," Christina replied. "I borrowed their washing machine."

"Didn't think of that," a red-faced Grant admitted.

Mount Vernon was already swarming with tourists when they arrived. Long lines of eager visitors waited to enter the Washingtons' home, kitchen, servant quarters and the other smaller, white outbuildings that surrounded the curious circle of grass in front of the mansion.

"Is it always this crowded?" Grant asked, nervous that so many people would see him in his "dandy" clothes.

"Mount Vernon's been open to the public for more than 140 years," Nellie said. "During that time, about 75 million people have visited."

"I guess that makes a lot of money for the Washingtons' ancestors," Grant said.

"The Washington family no longer owns Mount Vernon," Patrick explained. "The Mount Vernon Ladies Association purchased the estate in 1858 to save it for future generations to see."

"Interesting," Grant said like someone with something more pressing on his mind. "OK, who's ready to go with me to find Frank?"

"Oh, Grant," Christina said. "Haven't you taken that little prank far enough?"

"You'll be apologizing when I introduce Frank to you," Grant said. "Let's cut across this big pasture and see if we can find him where he was yesterday."

"Pasture?" Christina, Nellie, and Patrick asked in unison.

"Yeah," Grant answered. "The long stretch of grass in front of the mansion."

"That's no pasture," Christina said. "It's called a bowling green."

"Cool!" Grant said. "I didn't know George Washington liked to bowl."

"No, Grant," Christina explained. "It's just a pretty, open part of the landscape to give people a good view of the house when they approach."

"Guess that explains why there's no cow poop on it," Grant said with a grin.

Nellie giggled at Grant. "You're so funny," she said. "Even when you don't mean to be."

Christina was growing impatient. "OK, Grant, we'll go with you. I just hope you're not..."

The sound of someone hollering chopped off the end of her sentence. A tall, lanky man, trying to hold his hat on his head, chased what looked like a giant cotton ball with legs. "Make waaay!!!" he shouted. But it was too late. The giant cotton ball was charging straight at them!

7
PATRIOT GAMES

"Help!" Grant hollered. The angry sheep lowered his head and chose the back of Grant's gray breeches as a target.

POW! The sheep butted Grant's caboose and sent him flying head over heels in the soft grass. The man chasing the sheep apologized profusely. "So sorry," he said. "It's shearing time, and that ornery old sheep doesn't want to give up his wooly winter coat."

Grant stood, rubbing his bottom. "Guess he wanted my pants to wear with his coat!"

"Need some help herding him back to the barn?" Patrick asked.

"Yes!" the exasperated sheep shearer answered.

The kids shooed the sheep down a dirt path to reach the George Washington's Pioneer Farmer Site.

"Who lived in all these different houses?" Grant asked about the buildings lining the path.

"These aren't houses," Nellie said. "They were the different outbuildings Washington needed to run his plantation like a smokehouse, washhouse and coach house."

"I didn't know this was a plantation," Grant said.

"During the time Washington owned Mount Vernon, it was so large it was divided up into three different farms, and each had a separate overseer or boss," Patrick explained. "The farm here, where the Washingtons lived, was called Mansion House Farm."

Suddenly, the two-way radio in Patrick's pocket crackled to life. It was his mother. "I need you kids to report to the Hands on History tent," she said.

They waved goodbye to the sheep herder and headed for the tent set up near the mansion. Once there, they were immediately enlisted to participate in colonial games, including hide-and-seek. "I'm IT!" cried Grant, eager to play.

Christina slipped away from the others and made her way around the arched, covered walkway, called a palisade, that reached out from each side of the mansion like loving arms touching the servant's hall and kitchen. She tip-toed around the corner of the house and peeked at the long, wide porch lined with Windsor chairs. It was deserted except for one man. One man who looked a lot like George Washington!

Christina thought the man hadn't seen her. But when he said, "Come and join me, young lady!" she was so startled that she ran into the corner of the house and scraped her elbow. Christina crept cautiously toward the porch. Hadn't she just warned Grant about talking to strangers?

The George Washington look-a-like was peeling a Granny Smith apple with an old pocket knife. He stared into the distance as if daydreaming about some distant past. Christina looked across Mount Vernon's sloping backyard and could hardly believe her eyes. Large trees framed a wide river, flowing gently past the estate.

"Beautiful sight, isn't it?" the man asked, before crunching another slice of apple. Christina couldn't help but wonder if the real George could eat an apple with any of the clumsy, old sets of dentures he wore.

"I was proud to lead our nation to victory and proud to be the first president," the man continued. "But right here is where I loved to spend my time."

He noticed that Christina was staring at him as if she'd seen a ghost. "Sorry," he said. "Didn't mean to frighten you. I like to stay in character. I've been pretending to be George Washington for a long time here at Mount Vernon. Guess you could say George and I are kindred spirits. But I really enjoy acting as a re-enactor of the past."

"Say," he added, looking at Christina's elbow. "That's a nasty-looking scrape."

"These blocks are rough," Christina said, tapping the porch wall.

"That's one of Mount Vernon's many secrets," the re-enactor said. "The house looks like it's made from blocks, but those aren't blocks at all. The wooden siding is cut that way and then sand is thrown onto the wet paint to give it the texture of stone."

"Do you know any other secrets about Mount Vernon?" Christina asked hopefully.

"You know my first job was as a surveyor," the man said. "That's someone who uses special tools to measure distances, and such, and then draws maps or plans of how the land can best be used. I taught myself how to be a surveyor and started my own business when I was only 17 years old. I guess that's what made me design the circle in front of the house to be like a compass."

"So that's what that is!" Christina said in admiration.

"George" had already gone back inside when Grant, Patrick, and Nellie galloped onto the porch like a herd of excited horses.

"OK, OK," Christina said.   "You found me."

"No!" Grant said between gulps of breath. "We found another clue!"

8

SUNDOWN TO SUNUP

"Let me see!" Christina said excitedly.

Grant reached for his pants pocket to pull out the clue. "Oh, no!" Grant cried. "These pants don't even have a pocket! Where did people keep their stuff in the old days?"

"Grant, calm down!" said Nellie. "I have the clue in my hand." She handed Christina a piece of parchment similar to the one they found by the dentures.

"Weird," Christina said, reading the clue:

WORK LIKE A SLAVE
SUNDOWN TO SUNUP

"What could it mean, and, more importantly, who's leaving these clues?" Christina asked. "Where'd you find it?"

"Ha-Ha," said Grant.

"Grant, this is no laughing matter," Christina scolded with a look that said, "I'm the oldest, and I'm in charge while Mimi and Papa aren't here."

"I told you," Grant repeated. "Ha-Ha."

Patrick, who could see Christina's face and neck turning red with angry frustration, decided he'd better speak up. "Grant's telling the truth," he said. "We found the clue stuck in the Ha-Ha Wall."

"Never heard of it," said Christina, still annoyed. "Is that where you go to laugh it up?" Surely, these boys were pulling her leg.

"It does have a funny name," Nellie said. "But it's our favorite place to hide when we play hide-and-seek with the tourist kids."

Patrick explained, "The Ha-Ha Walls are sunken into the ground, so they're level with the lawn around the mansion. The other side is lower and keeps any cows, horses, or other animals in the pastures from messing up the grounds. It was another one of the clever things George Washington did to make this place so special."

"Sorry I didn't believe you, Grant," Christina apologized.

"It's OK, Tia," he said, using his nickname for her. "Now, where do we need to go to investigate that clue?"

Nellie made a suggestion. "Since it mentions a slave, maybe we should start at the slave quarters."

Christina lifted the corners of her skirt to reveal her silver sneakers. "I'm ready to run!" she said matter-of-factly.

Passing the greenhouse and then slinking along the brick wings that formed the slave quarters, the kids checked to make sure no tourists were nearby. Nellie motioned for them to follow as she crept into one of the rooms set up to show what a slave's life would have been like at Mount Vernon.

"Close the door, so we can plunder for clues without any nosy tourists asking questions," Patrick whispered.

A small fire in the fireplace cast shadows across the uneven brick floor.

"This is creepy," Grant said. "To think there were actually people kept as slaves here."

"Don't worry," Nellie said. "No slaves ever slept in this building. The original quarters burned down in 1835. A replica was constructed on the same foundation in the 1950s."

"It's still creepy," Grant said, patting the bunk bed filled with straw. "It's sad to think such a great American hero owned slaves to work in the fields."

"True," Patrick said. "Most of the slaves did work in the fields, but historians like our mother have found that many slaves had other important jobs. They were blacksmiths, carpenters, shoemakers, and weavers and were talented at many other skills to provide almost everything needed on the plantation. It couldn't have existed without them."

"Slavery was a terrible thing," Nellie added. "But George Washington was a fair master who, as he grew older and wiser, believed slavery was wrong. He wrote in his will that all his slaves were to be freed when his wife died."

Christina had already been poking around the room for clues. "See anything?" Grant asked.

"Not yet," Christina answered. She unrolled the clue and read it once again by the firelight. "I don't understand why it says slaves worked from sundown to sunup. Didn't most of them do just the opposite, work sunup to sundown?"

"Yep," Patrick answered. "Monday through Saturday."

"We've got two clues, if that's what they are, but, so far, I'm clueless," Christina said, thinking hard.

Suddenly, the door creaked as if to open. Was it the wind? Or had they been followed? Could it be Grant's man in the woods, Frank? What if it was the shadowy figure Christina had seen in the window? No matter who or what, all Christina could think was there's no place to run or hide!

9

SPECIAL SURPRISE?

"Mom!" Nellie and Patrick shouted as the door to the slave quarters fully opened.

"Don't know why, but I suspected you kids might be here," their mother said with a chuckle. "I've got another job for you. Remember, Grant and Christina, I said you'd have to earn your keep. Someone just radioed me that one of the tour boats will be docking soon at the wharf on the river. I want some cheerful colonial children there to greet it!"

Patrick gave his mother a suspicious look. "Why did you think we might be here?" he asked.

"I know this is one of the places you like to show friends," his mother answered.

Christina suddenly realized there was something she hadn't done. "Can you believe I've been at Mount Vernon all this time and I still haven't even been inside the house?"

Mrs. Tiller grinned slyly. "Why don't you save that tour for later," she said. "I've got a special surprise for you at supper. Besides," she added, "it's wall-to-wall tourists right now. You're here to work!"

The kids ambled down the South Lane. It was the same path they'd been on when they'd helped herd the angry sheep earlier. Now, the sun was high, and Grant was finding his dandy clothes more and more uncomfortable—as in hot and itchy.

"These ruffles are annoying," he said, pushing up his sleeves.

The birds seemed especially chattery, busy about their springtime chores of nest building and raising young. Christina couldn't help but wonder if they could be the offspring of the same birds that had sung for George and Martha Washington as they strolled the grounds.

"I can understand why this was Washington's favorite place to be," Christina said, admiring the neat rows of trees in the fruit garden.

"And just how do you know it was his favorite place?" Grant asked. "He lived a pretty exciting life, you know—he was a president and a general!"

"He told me this was his favorite spot," Christina said with a smile.

Grant was dumbfounded. "What?" he said. "You can't believe I talked with a soldier in the woods, but you expect me to believe you talked with Georgie, Porgie, Puddin' and Pie, himself?"

"He was really a re-enactor," Christina admitted sadly. "But it sure felt like I was talking to the real George Washington. I even think he wore false teeth."

"Did he have red hair like the young George Washington, or gray hair like the old George Washington?" Grant asked.

"He looked a lot like the one on the dollar bill, I guess," Christina said. "You know:

an old guy with a bad hair day. And he was more than six feet tall just like the real George Washington. He told me that he, George Washington, I mean, enjoyed his peaceful life with Martha here at Mount Vernon before the Revolutionary War began. His life here after the war was not as peaceful, since the entire country looked to him as a great leader and many people wanted him to be president. After he served as president for eight years, he only got to live here for two years before he died."

"That's sad," Grant said.

"At least he got to be buried here," Christina said.

"He is?" Grant asked, surprised.

"He and Martha, both," Christina said. "We'll be sure and visit their tombs before we leave."

Grant glanced over his shoulder at Patrick and Nellie, who were lagging behind and whispering to each other. "Did you figure something out?" Grant asked.

"We have a theory about who could be leaving the notes," Nellie said. "Our mother."

"Yeah," Patrick agreed. "She's probably just leading us on some kind of educational scavenger hunt. That's how she knew we were at the slave quarters, and she's the only one who knows how much we like to hide behind the Ha-Ha Walls. Why would anyone else hide a note there?"

"Maybe you're right," Christina agreed. "She did say she had a special surprise for us. Maybe she's got a reward for us if we solve her clues."

Three short toots from the tourist boat spurred the kids into a trot. Most of the tourists waved happily as the four kids in colonial garb greeted them.

One boy stuck his tongue out at Christina. "I've never seen a girl from George Washington's day wearing sneakers," he shouted rudely.

Christina bit her tongue and waved at him pleasantly. She was on "official duty," after all, and had to stay "in character," like it or not!

When the tourists debarked and streamed toward the mansion, the boat pulled away from the dock. The kids waved the captain off and then stood and enjoyed the quiet shoreline.

SPLASH, SPLASH, SPLASH! "What was that?" Grant asked as a stone whizzed past them and skipped across the flowing water.

A twig snapped in the grove of trees behind them, and everyone froze. Someone was watching them! Or were they under attack? WHIZ! WHIZZ! OUCH!

10
TALL, DARK AND SNEAKY

Christina peered into the shadows cast by the large trees. "I don't see anyone," she whispered. "But someone certainly sees us."

Each of the kids was tense and ready to run when Christina saw movement. A tall, dark figure stalked cautiously toward the tree line but stopped before stepping out into the sunlight.

Christina couldn't believe her ears when a deep voice asked, "Grant, is that you?" To her surprise, Grant answered. "Frank?"

"Yeah, it's me," the deep voice answered back.

"Well, well, well," Grant crowed. "Looks like we don't have to go looking for my friend Frank. He's found us. Come on out and meet my sister and friends," Grant yelled to the shadowy figure.

"Got a great place to sit under the trees," Frank answered. "Come on in."

Christina didn't say anything, but her look told Grant, "We really shouldn't."

"He's a nice guy—really," Grant assured his sister and headed into the tree grove.

"Graaant!" Christina called after him. "Oh brother, I can't let him go alone," she told Patrick and Nellie. "There's strength in numbers. Will you go with me?"

"Sure," Patrick said like a brave soldier. Grant and Frank were already seated on a fallen log. Christina could see the glint of Frank's knife. He pulled its sharp edge along the length of a stick, sending curls of light-colored wood spiraling to the ground around his well-worn boots. As her eyes adjusted from the bright sunlight to the shadowy woods, she could see he was indeed dressed like a Revolutionary War soldier—a raggedy soldier like those they'd seen on the interactive movie.

"So, what have you kids been up to at Mount Vernon?" he asked with a smile that showed a mouthful of teeth that looked like they hadn't seen a brush in weeks. Christina was thankful Grant was sitting beside him and not her. She could only imagine how bad his breath smelled.

"Have you found anything interesting?" Frank asked.

Christina held her breath and hoped her brother would keep quiet. He didn't.

"Only a couple of clues," Grant said.

Christina used her sharp elbow to give her brother a hard punch in the ribs.

"Ouch!" they said in unison. Christina had forgotten about her nasty elbow scrape from the mansion siding. Grant grabbed his side in pain.

"I know what you're thinking," Grant said. "But we can trust Frank. Besides, the clues may only be a prank from Nellie and Patrick's mom."

Another wood curl flew off Frank's whittling stick. "Sure, you can trust me," he said with a friendly nod. "There's nothing I love better than a good mystery."

"Why haven't we ever seen you around here?" Nellie blurted out. Patrick gave her the same kind of look Christina had given Grant.

"I'm surprised you've never seen me," he said. "I've certainly seen the two of you around. Your mother's Mrs. Tiller, right?"

Patrick and Nellie nodded and looked relieved that Frank was a real person who knew their mother.

"I spend most of my time on the edges of the estate to help lost tourists," Frank continued. "It's a lonely job sometimes, but someone has to do it."

"Why do you wear that uniform?" Christina asked.

Frank looked down at his badly worn shoes and brushed the wood chips off his dirty, patched pants. "I guess a fancy, clean uniform would look a lot better," he admitted. "But the truth is, most of the soldiers who fought under General George Washington were a ragtag bunch. They were simple farmers and merchants. They were not 'fancy pants'."

Grant wiggled self-consciously in his dandy outfit. "Wanna see our clues?" he asked Frank.

"Sure!" Frank replied eagerly. Maybe even greedily, Christina thought. She fished the slips of parchment out of her sneakers, where she had placed them for safekeeping.

"Ewww!" Grant said, holding his nose. "These are some stinky clues!"

Christina turned as red as a British soldier's coat. "My feet don't stink!" she exclaimed.

Frank laughed. "It's OK, Christina. I'm sure your feet don't smell as bad as mine."

He opened the parchment scrolls and studied them carefully. "Interesting," he said. "I wouldn't doubt there's another set of Washington's teeth somewhere on this plantation. Wouldn't that be a wonderful historic find?"

"And fetch a bundle of 'Washingtons'!" Grant added.

"What do you make of the other clue?" Patrick asked eagerly.

Frank pulled at the short whiskers on his chin. "This one's tough," he said. "Especially since it's backwards from what you think it would be."

"That's what I said!" Christina agreed. Maybe this Frank guy was OK.

"A lot of slave work involved working in the fields," Frank continued. "That included hoeing long crop rows of tobacco, corn, and all kinds of vegetables. Since the sun rises in the east and sets in the west, maybe this means working west to east. My suggestion would be to go to the Pioneer Farm. They're always looking for volunteers to hoe a row or two—which is one reason I never go over there!"

The sudden sound of voices coming from the shoreline caused Frank to stand up quickly. "Guess I better go," he said. "Let me know what you find!"

The kids watched as Frank shuffled deeper into the shadows. Christina couldn't help herself. She was suspicious.

11

HARD ROW TO HOE

HAW-Heeee, HAW-Heeee, He, He, Heeeee...HAW-Heeee, HAW-Heeee, He, He, Heeeee!

Christina and Grant stopped in their tracks. "What in the world is that!?" Christina asked.

Grant pulled off his gray wig, ran his fingers through his sweaty blonde curls, and plopped the wig back on his head like a baseball cap. "Oh, I know," he said. "It's probably a tourist having a good laugh at my costume."

Nellie snickered. "I'm afraid you're not much of a farm boy, Grant," she said. "That's no tourist."

"It's a donkey, right?" Christina asked, pointing to the large, gray animal watching them approach the pioneer farm.

"Only partly," Patrick replied. "It's half donkey and half horse—it's a mule."

"It's the same color as the one we always see General Washington riding in our text books," Grant said. "But I thought Washington rode horses, not mules."

"He did keep horses to ride and pull buggies," Patrick explained. "Washington was athletic and an excellent horseman. He had several favorite horses. The big gray you mentioned was Blueskin. Nelson was another favorite. They served with Washington during the Revolutionary War and got to retire to Mount Vernon when it was over."

"That's so cool!" Christina said. "But what are the mules for?"

"Washington was a farmer at heart," Nellie said. "He was always trying new things and trying to find better ways of doing things. He found that mules were better work animals than horses and helped make them popular in the new country."

Christina looked at Grant to make sure he was listening to this interesting bit of history. He wasn't. His eyes were as big as Mimi's pancakes. Christina turned to see what had him so mesmerized.

"Uh, oh," she muttered when she saw.

"Run for your lives!" Grant hollered.

The same sheep that had used Grant as a bullseye in front of the mansion was on the loose again. This time, he was even angrier. He looked like a skinny streaker. His wooly coat was sheared except for two strips along his side that fluttered in the wind like tassels on a kid's bike handles.

Each of them ran in a different direction, but once again, the sheep picked Grant as his target. Grant dove for cover behind a split-rail fence and instead landed right on top of the rough wood.

CRASH! The angry sheep slammed on his brakes and looked at Grant like, "You're in big trouble now, buddy!"

The lanky sheep herder tiptoed up to the distracted sheep and tackled him like a linebacker. "Got you now, trouble maker!" he cried triumphantly. "Back to the pasture, and next year, find yourself a different barber!"

Grant moaned and slowly pulled himself to his feet. "Being a farm boy is dangerous business!" he said.

Christina, Patrick, and Nellie laughed. "It wasn't that funny," Grant said.

"Sorry, Grant," Nellie said. "It's just that your ponytail is hanging over your ear!"

"Ugh," Grant sighed, twisting the wig back into position.

Soon, the farm overseer was surveying the damage. "We'd like to make it up to you," Christina said sweetly. "Looks like you've got several weedy rows that could use hoeing."

"Yessss," he said. "That's a great idea. Those English peas certainly need tending, and I've got a sow about to give birth to a litter of pigs. I'll get the hoes while you re-stack this fence."

The kids remembered Frank's suggestion and worked west to east along the rows. With each chop into the rich brown soil, Christina hoped to pull up a clue as well as a weed. But when the others reached the end of their rows before her without striking pay dirt, she was discouraged.

"Hurry, Christina," Grant fussed. "It's been soooo long since breakfast, and I'm starving!"

"Almost done!" Christina promised. She took aim at a particularly tall and evil-looking weed with a big chop. CLANK!

Vibration from the impact traveled up the wooden hoe handle, up Christina's arms, and raced around her mouth, rattling her teeth.

The others noticed Christina had stopped. "What wrong?" Nellie asked.

Christina answered, "I've either found a clanking weed, or I've found a clue!"

12

BURIED TREASURE!

The kids kneeled around Christina and helped her dig. All their hands were muddy when Christina pulled a small, rusty metal box from the ground.

"Wow!" Grant exclaimed. "Maybe that's not a clue; maybe there's a set of teeth in there."

Before they had the chance to find out, the kids realized the overseer was walking toward them. Christina quickly tried to find a place to hide the box. "How did kids carry things in the olden days?" she whispered, frantically searching for a pocket. The box was too big to fit in her shoe. Suddenly, she had an idea. She lifted Grant's wig by its ponytail and plopped the box on Grant's head underneath. Grant shot Christina an angry look. "Shhhh!" she cautioned.

"You kids did a great job," the overseer said. "Find a stubborn weed you had to pull out by hand?"

"Yep!" Christina said. "It was a mean one."

Grant scratched his head nervously. "Have the pigs been born?" he asked.

"She had 15!" the overseer said proudly.

"That's a lot of bacon!" Grant said.

"Graaant!" Christina cried in disgust. "They're only babies."

"He's right, though," the overseer said. "The Washingtons and everyone else who lived here depended on hogs, sheep, chickens, and fish from the river for food. There were no grocery stores or drive-through restaurants back then. They had to catch or grow everything they ate."

"I know of one sheep I would like to see on my plate as a lamb chop!" Grant said.

"Graaant!" the girls cried again.

"We've got lots of baby animals if you'd like to come and see them," the overseer offered.

"Maybe later," Christina said.

"Yeah," Grant agreed. "All this talk of food has my stomach growling like a mad dog!"

Nellie had an idea. "Why don't we go up to the kitchen and see if they're cooking hoecakes today?" she said. "Do you know what hoecakes are?"

"Course we do!" Christina said, offended. "We're Southern kids from Georgia, remember? Mimi has told us about how people working in the fields would mix cornmeal, water and salt into little cakes and cook them over a fire on their hoes."

"Well, did you also know that George Washington loved to eat hoecakes slathered with butter?" Patrick asked.

"Didn't know that," Christina admitted. "I figured his favorite was something fancier than that."

The kids scurried up the path until Patrick waved them to follow him onto a side trail. It didn't take long before they reached a circular brick structure surrounding a gray stone shaft, dedicated to the memory of the African Americans who served as slaves at Mount Vernon.

Grant looked around to make sure no one was there to see. Then, he took the wig off his head and the box underneath. "Talk about a bee in your bonnet," he said. "A metal box is much worse."

Nellie couldn't resist the opportunity to tease her new friend. "Oh, Grant," she said in a mocking tone. "I didn't know you liked to wear bonnets, too."

Grant snickered. "Guess I asked for that one, didn't I?" he said.

Christina took the box from Grant and tried to open the lid. "Seems to be stuck," she said.

"Step aside," Grant said. He set the box on its side, pulled the plastic hatchet from his waistband, and gave the box a whack. It spun like a top, wobbled, and then popped open like a clam. A small, parchment scroll rolled onto the bricks.

"Awww!" Grant said, disappointed. "It's not teeth!"

Christina carefully unrolled the paper as the others crowded around her for a glimpse. She read aloud:

32 NORTH, 14 EAST, 5 SOUTH.

"No way your mother's leaving clues this hard," Christina said before she tucked the scroll in her shoe. She pushed her fingers into her hair and pressed her temples with her palms like she could squeeze the answer from her brain.

She wondered, what can this mean?

13

CLUE OR KNOT?

"Take a right up there," Nellie told Grant.

"You don't have to give him directions to food," Christina assured her. "He's following his nose."

Grant made a beeline to the kitchen house near the mansion where staff members were giving out hoecakes just like the ones George Washington had once enjoyed. "Can we sit in the green circle?" Grant asked Patrick. He wanted to have an afternoon picnic in the perfectly round spot of grass in front of the mansion.

"We're really not supposed to, but since we're in costume, we'll just become part of a display—colonial kids enjoying a snack!" said Patrick, leading the way.

Grant balanced a stack of hoecakes on his hand and sat down, criss-cross applesauce on the soft grass.

"How'd you manage to get five?" Christina asked him.

Grant smiled. "I just used my boyish charm," he said.

Christina took a bite of buttery hoecake, crunchy on the outside—warm and gooey on the inside. "Mmmm," she said. "Scrumptious!"

When he'd finished gobbling his snack, Grant wiped his mouth on his fancy shirtsleeve. Then he yawned, stretched out in the warm sun, and patted his belly. "I could get used to life at Mount Vernon," he said.

After several minutes of staring at the clouds, Grant sat up suddenly. "Hey, I just thought of something," he said. "Why is this place called Mount Vernon and not Mount Washington? I mean, it's weird that our nation's capital was named in his honor and his own home was not."

"I guess I never thought of that," Christina said. "That's a good question."

Patrick stood up and started pacing like a tour guide.

"Uh, oh," Nellie said. "This may be a long answer."

"Let me tell you the history of Mount Vernon," Patrick said in a deep voice. "It was George Washington's great-grandfather who first owned 5,000 acres of land here on the Potomac River in the late 1600s. His father, Augustine, bought part of the property from his sister, and George was born on a plantation on Pope's Creek in 1732. When George was three years old, his family moved to the Hunting Creek Plantation. George's older half-brother, Lawrence, inherited that property.

"Now, listen carefully to this part," Patrick added, wagging his finger. "Lawrence had served in the British Navy and decided to rename his plantation in honor of his commander. Guess what his name was? It was Admiral Edward Vernon. And since the estate is on a hill..."

"Or Mount," Christina chimed in.

"Yep," Patrick finished. "That's where the name, Mount Vernon, came from."

Grant raised his hand like he was in school. "But when did George Washington become the owner?" he asked.

"George lived here as a boy with his half-brother and sister-in-law after his father died. After they died, he inherited the estate," Patrick explained.

"How cool would it be to inherit a mansion like this!" Grant said.

Patrick shook his head. "It wasn't a mansion then," he said. "Historians believe George's father built a simple house here. Lawrence probably made it larger. But it was George who turned it into a mansion."

Christina clapped her hands. "You sure know a lot about this place," she said.

Patrick bowed. "Someday, I plan to be a historian like my mother," he said. "Who knows, maybe I'll get a job at Mount Vernon."

"Hey!" Grant shouted. "Look at this! I have a shadow crawling up my leg." Christina studied the thin shadow leaving its mark on her brother. "It's coming from that thing in the middle of the circle," she said, scrambling to her feet to investigate.

"That's a sundial," Nellie said with a giggle as Grant squirmed away from the shadow. It's one of the ways people told time in colonial days."

Grant, arms outstretched, ran around the circle. "Tick, tock, tick, tock," he chortled. "Look at me. I'm part of a clock!"

Christina leaned on the sundial and began slowly turning and counting the posts surrounding the grass circle with her finger. "It's a clock all right," she said. "But it's also a compass! That's it! The George I talked with on the back porch told me that George Washington made this like a compass. This is where we need to figure out our clue!"

After Christina had fished the clue out of her shoe for review, she asked, "Where do we start? The first part says 32 NORTH. Which way is north?"

"I know the sun rises over the river," Patrick said. "Toward Piscataway."

"Piscatawhat?" Christina asked.

"It's the national forest across the river from Mount Vernon," Patrick said, pointing in that direction.

Grant giggled. "Yeah," he said. "Piscataway is thataway!"

Christina and Patrick rolled their eyes, but Nellie giggled at Grant's rhyme.

"Anyway," Patrick continued, "since that way is east, north is that way." He pointed in a different direction.

"Go and stand in front of that post, Grant," Christina commanded. "The next part of the clue says, 14 EAST."

Christina carefully counted 14 posts back toward the east. "Now, move there, Grant," she said and pointed. "Now, one more time, move five posts toward the south."

"I feel like one of those little wooden men that pop out of a clock and march around," Grant whined when he reached the post. "You're not gonna make me say cuckoo are you?"

Christina ignored his silly comment and stared at the post. "If this is what the clue meant, there must be something special about this post," she said. "But what?"

Grant looked on all sides of the post. "Don't see any clues nailed to it," he said. "Could it be buried underneath it?"

"I think they're set in concrete," Patrick said. "And the grass is undisturbed. I don't think anyone's been digging around here."

Christina dropped to her hands and knees to give the post a close inspection. She noticed a knothole in the wood. When she pushed it with her finger, it wiggled slightly!

A curious tourist stopped to ask if anything was wrong. "Post inspection," Patrick said with authority, and the tourist nodded and moved on.

"I need something sharp to pry it out," Christina said.

"Try this," Nellie offered. She had removed a buckle from her shoe.

After several attempts, the knothole popped out like a cork. Christina cautiously used her finger to probe inside. "I think I feel something!" she said. "Maybe another clue!"

14
FEATHERED MUMMIES

"OUCH!" Christina yelped. "Something bit me!"

"Was it a wasp?" Nellie asked, worried. "No," Christina said, still poking her finger in the hole. "It didn't feel like a sting." Slowly, Christina raked something to the edge of the hole and cupped her other hand underneath to catch what she'd found. *Plip!* A small, white object landed in her palm.

"Let me see!" Grant begged.

"What is it?" Patrick asked.

"It's...It's...a...t-t-t...tooth!" Christina stuttered.

"You're kidding!" Patrick exclaimed, bending down for a closer look.

Grant was impressed but curious. "How did one tooth bite you?" he asked.

Christina turned the tooth over and examined it carefully. "This is not just an ordinary tooth," she said. "See? There's a tiny screw at the bottom. I think that's what hurt my finger. And it looks like this tooth came out of a set of old false teeth!"

"Maybe there's more in the hole," Grant said. He poked his finger inside, fishing furiously and sticking his tongue out. That was a sure sign that Grant was trying his hardest.

"Got it!" he said.

"Is it another tooth?" Nellie asked.

"Looks like another clue," Grant said, wiggling a small square of parchment from the hole. He unfolded it and read to the others:

YOU'VE FOUND ONE, BUT YOU'RE NOT DONE! FIRST IN WAR, FIRST IN PEACE, AND FIRST IN THE HEARTS OF HIS COUNTRYMEN. FOLLOW THE SUN TO FIND GEORGE WASHINGTON.

"Another clue about following the sun?" Grant moaned. "I'm too tired to do any more hoeing!"

"I don't think this clue has anything to do with working in the fields," said Christina. "'First in war, first in peace, and first in the hearts of his countrymen' was a popular saying about Washington. I remember reading that in school. It means he was number one because he won the Revolutionary War. He was number one because he became the first president when peace returned and our country was an independent nation. And, of course, he's still number one in our hearts. I mean, look at how many people come here to learn about him!"

"If we follow the sun, we'll go west," Patrick reminded them.

"That's right," Christina said. "And aren't the Washingtons' sarcophagi that way?"

"Yes!" Patrick said.

"Now, wait a minute," Grant protested. "Why are you saying sarcophagi? Is that the same thing as a sarcophagus?"

"Yes," Christina explained. "Sarcophagi is the plural of sarcophagus. There are two of them. One for George, and one for Martha."

"But aren't those the things mummies come out of?" Grant asked. "Are you saying that they made mummies out of George and Martha?" He shuddered.

"No, Grant," Christina said, trying to be patient and remember her younger brother didn't know as much as she knew. "Their bodies are just inside stone coffins. They weren't mummified like the Egyptians."

"Still sounds creepy," Grant mumbled.

The kids galloped full speed down the tomb road when a loud whistle startled them near the path marked Forest Trail.

"Should we check it out?" Christina asked.

"Naaa," Patrick answered. "Probably just a bird."

"Or a mummy?" Grant added.

The kids started walking again, but another whistle split the air. This time in three short blasts.

"That's no bird," Christina said. "I think someone on the Forest Trail is trying to get our attention!"

Warily, the kids turned down the trail. The new green leaves of the forest were the color of lime, and tiny wildflowers in pinks and purples poked their heads through last year's leaves on the forest floor.

Despite the forest's beauty, Grant wasn't taking any chances. He pulled out his hatchet and held it in chopping position. They hadn't gone far when—WHOOSH!! Something came at them out of the woods. They all covered their faces with their arms. Grant wildly swung his hatchet.

"Mummies!" he cried. "They're after us!"

Christina heard the rush of powerful wings and peeked between her elbows. "It's OK, Grant!" she shouted. "They'll be gone soon."

After several seconds the woods were peaceful again. Grant grabbed his chest and sank to his knees in exhaustion. "Thank goodness I had my hatchet to scare those mummies away," he said. "They were gigantic."

Nellie and Patrick burst into laughter. "Mount Vernon isn't going to be nearly as fun after you leave, Grant," Nellie said.

"Yeah," Patrick agreed between laughs. "Not many people could mistake wild turkeys for mummies."

"Those didn't look like any turkeys I've ever seen," Grant said.

"That's what they look like before they become the giant, plastic-covered balls Mimi buys at the grocery store," Christina said. "But thanks for being brave enough to protect us!"

A short distance later, the kids could see someone pacing on a wooden bridge. CLOMP, CLOMP, CLOMP. As they drew closer, the person stopped. He pointed a rifle at them and shouted. "Halt! Who goes there?!"

15
WINGS OF WOOD

The kids reached for the sky and shouted as one, "Don't shoot!"

"Don't worry," a familiar voice consoled them. "I carved this gun out of wood. It couldn't shoot a thing. Just makes me look **authentic**."

It was Frank! "When I heard kids on the road, I was hoping it was you," he said. "Glad you heard my whistle."

Grant looked at his plastic hatchet and then looked at Frank's wooden gun. "Could you carve me a gun like that?" he asked.

"I don't know, Grant," Frank said. "It might get you into too much trouble."

Christina nodded in agreement.

"But I did carve something for you," Frank said. "In fact, I have a little gift for each of you."

Frank propped his fake gun against the bridge's handrail and pulled a little muslin bag from his raggedy pants pocket. It was the kind of bag a Revolutionary soldier might have used to carry his gunpowder or other supplies. He pulled the drawstring with his dirty teeth and then reached in and pulled out four small objects, handing one to each of the children.

"Frank, it's beautiful," Christina said as she admired an American eagle carved from wood.

"I carved them out of oak," Frank said. "That's the official national tree, you know."

"And the eagle is another symbol of our nation," Grant added.

"That's right, Grant," Frank said. "But did you know some of the founding fathers wanted the national bird to be the turkey?"

"Boy!" Grant exclaimed. "I'm glad they didn't do that. Those wild turkeys are too scary!"

"Here's a string," Frank said, handing each of them a black cord. "Thought you might like to wear your carvings around your neck."

"Great!" Christina said. "I don't have any place else to put it, and this tooth is already killing me." Christina clamped her hand over her mouth. She had not planned on telling anyone about the tooth until they'd talked with Nellie and Patrick's mother, Mrs. Tiller.

"Sorry to hear you have a toothache," Frank said. "My teeth bother me a lot, too." Christina wanted to suggest a toothbrush to help his problem but decided against being rude, especially since he'd given them such a beautiful gift.

"Oh, Christina doesn't have a toothache," Grant blurted. "We found another clue, and she has a tooth in her shoe!"

Leave it to Grant to spill the beans or, in this case, the teeth, Christina thought.

"Well, my goodness," said Frank. "I've heard of someone putting their foot in their mouth but never putting their mouth in their foot!"

"Good one, Frank," Grant said with a chuckle.

"So what did this clue say?" Frank asked. "Did you figure it out yet?"

Grant read the clue to Frank and said, "We're going to see the sarcophaguses."

"Sarcophagi," Christina corrected.

"Sounds like you're on the right track," said Frank. "In fact, there's an eagle on Washington's sarcophagus that looks a lot like the ones I carved for you. Take a close look and see if you agree."

Grant gave Christina a "what are you waiting for" look and said, "Go ahead, Christina, show him the tooth."

Reluctantly, Christina slipped off her shoe and pulled out the tooth that had been poking her in the foot. Frank offered a metal cup clipped to his belt, and she dropped the tooth in it. To Christina's surprise, it made a dull thud. Not the clank you'd expect from a tooth.

Furrows formed in Frank's brow, and he stroked his whiskers. "You know, this looks like it could be an artifact," he said. "You kids could get into a heap of trouble if anyone found out you were tampering with artifacts. Why don't you let me take care of this? I'll make sure it gets to the right people."

"We'll just give it to our mother," Patrick said. "She'll know what to do."

Frank shook his head. "Bad idea," he said. "That might get you and your mother in big trouble. She might even lose her job. We certainly don't want that to happen, now do we?"

Christina could see tears welling in Nellie's eyes. "Of course not!" Nellie cried. "Our mother loves her job!"

"Don't worry," Frank said in a comforting voice. "You just let old Frank take care of this. You just keep on doing what you're doing; and when you find something else, bring it to me and everything will be OK."

Christina noticed that Patrick was patting his sides with a panicked look on his face. "What's wrong, Patrick?" she asked.

"I just realized I've lost my two-way radio," he said. "I'm sure Mom's tried to call. Finding artifacts may be the least of our worries when she gets hold of us."

"Thanks, Frank!" the kids all yelled with a wave as they headed out of the forest. They hadn't gone far when Christina turned to give Frank another goodbye wave. It was too late. He had already disappeared. She couldn't help but wonder if what they had done was what would really end up getting them in trouble!

16
ENTOMBED

The kids decided they had just enough time to visit the Washingtons' final resting place before supper. Patrick said that's when his mother would really start to worry.

With the sun beginning to sink in the west, the tomb was a quiet and peaceful place. Towering oak trees stood like faithful soldiers guarding the grave of their commander. American flags fluttered on each side of the closed iron gates that were set inside a huge brick arch.

There might not even be an American flag if George Washington had never lived, Christina thought. She pulled on one of the gates until it creaked open wide enough for them to enter.

Grant was still nervous. "Are you sure we should be doing this?" he asked. "Those gates were probably closed for a reason. You might let something out that shouldn't be let out."

"What's the matter?" Nellie teased. "Would you like to borrow my name for a while?"

"What's that supposed to mean?" Grant asked.

"Then you could be a nervous Nellie!" she answered with a chuckle.

"Not funny," Grant complained.

Christina slid through the opening but hesitated with the feeling that she wasn't alone. Maybe Grant's fear of the tomb was rubbing off on her. Christina could see that a fresh green wreath with a black ribbon decorated each sarcophagus. She did a double-take when she noticed that the wreath on Martha Washington's tomb appeared to be moving. With a gasp, Christina stepped out of the enclosure and quickly slammed the gate.

"Maybe this isn't a good idea," she said, still peering through the iron bars.

When a furry, little head popped up out of the middle of the wreath, Christina exhaled a deep breath in relief. "Only a squirrel," she said. "Follow me."

Christina opened the gate again, and they filed inside.

"Is he really in there?" Grant said, staring somberly at Washington's tomb. "The real George Washington?"

"He really is," Christina said. "I'm glad he's getting to rest in peace at Mount Vernon. Now, everyone look for clues; the light is fading fast."

After several minutes of searching revealed nothing, Grant pulled up his eagle necklace for a closer look. "Wow!" he said. "The eagle on Washington's sarcophagi does look a lot like the eagles Frank carved for us!"

"One is a sarcophagus!" Christina said, doubtful that her brother would ever get it right. "Two or more are sarchophagi, got it, big guy?"

Christina rubbed her hands over the stone eagle. Its head stood out from the lid in three- dimensional relief. When Christina felt the back of the eagle's head, her eyes grew wide. Stuck behind the head was another tooth and parchment clue!

"I don't believe it!" Christina exclaimed. She strained to read the words in the purple twilight:

FIND THE KEY AND YOU WILL SEE THE PLACE THESE TEETH ARE MEANT TO BE.

"Nice rhyme!" Grant said. "We better get this tooth to Frank, and maybe he can help us figure out what the clue means."

"Do you really want to go walking in those woods at night?" Christina questioned.

"Well..." Grant began.

C-R-E-A-K! Before Grant could finish his sentence, the iron gate slammed shut. Christina grabbed it and shook it hard. To her horror, it wouldn't open. They were trapped! Christina realized for the first time that she was mixed up in a mystery of historic proportions. Mimi and Papa always scolded her and Grant for getting themselves in "fixes" as Papa called them. But their grandparents were always at hand to bail them out if they got into trouble. This time, Mimi and Papa were miles away in Washington, D.C. Now, she wondered, who was going to bail them out this time?

17
PASSAGE TO SURPRISE

What could be scarier than being locked in George and Martha Washington's tomb? Being locked in George and Martha Washington's tomb with a floating, scary-looking, white blob quickly approaching!

"I kn-kn-knew this was a b-b-b-bad i-d-d-dea," Grant stuttered. "It's h-h-headed right f-f-f-for us!"

The white blob was bouncing along the trail, sometimes seeming to float and hover among the trees.

"Help me, quick!" Christina said.

All four kids shook the gate with all their might. It wouldn't budge. But the noise made the white blob stop.

"Looks like we're trapped," Christina said. "Hide!"

Christina and Grant cowered behind George's sarcophagus, while Nellie and Patrick crouched behind Martha's.

To their surprise, they heard feet click-clacking on the brick outside the gate.

"I didn't know ghosts wore shoes," Grant whispered.

The white blob slipped through the iron bars and whirred around the tomb. Finally, Christina realized it wasn't a blob at all. It was only a light. Still, she wasn't convinced that the person carrying it had not locked them in to do them harm.

"Paaaaatrick!" a woman's voice called. "Neeeeellie!"

Patrick and Nellie popped up like corks that had been held under water. "Mom!" they screamed. "We're in here!"

"Are Christina and Grant with you?" she asked.

Sheepishly, Christina and Grant stood up and shielded their eyes from the blinding beam of light.

"Do you have any idea how worried I've been?" Mrs. Tiller asked angrily. "Patrick, I've been calling your radio for hours."

"Sorry, Mom," he said. "I think I may have left it at the Pioneer Farm Site earlier today."

"Have you forgotten that I said I had a special treat I'd tell you about at dinner?" she asked.

Before they had a chance to answer, Mrs. Tiller continued in the rapid-fire way that mothers can. "Well, dinner is growing cold. What are you kids doing in there after dark, anyway? I thought hide-and-seek ended hours ago."

"It did," Nellie admitted. "We were just showing Christina and Grant the tombs when someone locked us in."

Mrs. Tiller seemed skeptical. "Someone locked you in here?" she asked.

"Yes," Patrick said. "We can't open the gate."

Mrs. Tiller pushed the gate handle, fully expecting it to open. "That's odd," she said, perplexed. Keys jangled like Christmas bells as Mrs. Tiller tried key after key on a large ring that held all shapes and sizes to fit locks all over the estate. Finally, the kids heard the lock tumblers move as she turned the correct key.

"I'll bet it was a *skeleton* key that did the trick," Grant whispered to his sister.

Patrick and Nellie bear-hugged their mother like they hadn't seen her in years. Grant and Christina gave each other a relieved high-five.

"I'm glad you kids are OK," Mrs. Tiller said, still not quite believing that someone could have actually locked the kids inside the tomb area. But she couldn't take any chances. "I'll tell the maintenance people this lock needs changing—right away."

After an extremely eventful day, Christina didn't feel she needed another surprise. But she did need dinner. And when they were hiding, she had heard her always-hungry brother's stomach rumbling loud enough to, well, to wake the dead.

When they reached the mansion—the mansion that Christina still had not been inside—they were all surprised to see lights gleaming in the darkness. Christina looked expectantly at the upstairs window where she'd seen a shadowy figure. Nothing.

The next surprise was when Mrs. Tiller led them to the front door.

"Welcome to Mount Vernon!" she said and swung the great, red door open wide before waving them inside with a flourish. "Please wipe your feet!"

Christina could practically smell the history oozing out of this majestic place. The Washingtons and many other important historic legends had walked on these floors. These walls had heard their conversations and kept their secrets. These walls had listened as they laughed, cried, and prayed during the birth of a new nation—her nation— the United States of America. It gave her cold chills just to think of it all.

Christina could imagine George Washington stamping into the house after visiting the stables to see a prized new foal being born or checking on the progress of the summer vegetable garden. She could imagine his stepchildren, John Parke and Martha Parke Custis, running to greet him as his wife, Martha, scolded him for tracking mud on the floor. For the first time, she could see George Washington as more than a name in her history book or the face on a dollar bill. She could see him as a real and living person.

"Something smells awesome!" Grant said, interrupting Christina's thoughts. Christina wanted to tell him it was the wonderful smell of hundreds of years of history. But she knew he wouldn't understand.

Mrs. Tiller led them into the home's wide central hall, known as the Passage. Christina could see that it ran straight through the center of the house to a large set of double doors. The doors were closed, but she knew they opened onto the piazza, or porch, where she had visited with the George Washington re-enactor earlier in the day.

A single candle shined from a square, glass fixture hanging from the ceiling and cast eerie shadows on the dark, wood-paneled walls and the staircase.

"This is where the Washingtons enjoyed entertaining guests," Mrs. Tiller explained. "Especially during the summer, when they would open the back door and let the cool breezes from the river flow through the house."

"Is this paneling made from oak?" Grant asked, assuming that Washington would choose the national tree for his woodwork.

"Good guess, Grant," Mrs. Tiller said. "But this paneling is just one of the many special secrets in the house. It's really pine, but George Washington had craftsmen use a technique called 'graining' so that it would look like a much more expensive wood called mahogany."

Patrick and Nellie, who had both been inside the mansion hundreds of times, ran ahead and disappeared through a doorway. By the time Christina, Grant, and Mrs. Tiller caught up with them, they were standing at the doorway of a large room with their mouths agape.

"SURPRISE!" Mrs. Tiller yelled.

18
IN OR OUT?

Christina rubbed her eyes. What she thought was the smell of history was actually a scrumptious dinner fit for a king or, in this case, a famous first president.

"How'd this get here?" Patrick asked, incredulous.

"Yeah!" Nellie exclaimed. "I've never seen food in here before."

"Well it *is* a dining room," Mrs. Tiller said with a smile.

Christina looked around the room in wonder. She could tell it was a dining room. A long table large enough for at least a dozen people sat before a huge Palladian window that in the daytime must have flooded the room with light, she thought. But tonight, candlesticks on the table joined forces with candles mounted to sconces with mirrors behind them to throw a magical, flickering glow around the room.

Christina admired the green walls that reached to a ceiling that she had to crane her neck back to see. Fancy, white, plaster decorations stood out from the green walls like the swirls of frosting on a wedding cake. In the decorations, Christina could see crops and tools—things that Washington loved. Paintings of country scenes also decorated the walls.

Grant was more interested in the food than in the room. "Who cares how the food got here?" he said, sniffing. "Let's eat!"

Each of them sat down to shallow bowls of a tan-colored soup. The steam tickled Christina's nose, and although the soup looked unlike anything she'd ever eaten, it smelled like something familiar.

Grant must have been thinking the same thing. "This smells like a peanut butter sandwich," he said, wrinkling his nose.

"It should," Mrs. Tiller said. "It's peanut soup." The other dishes needed no explanation. There was roast turkey, cornbread stuffing, cranberry sauce, and English peas like the ones they'd hoed in the garden. And dessert, of course, was cherry pie.

Stuffed with the colonial cuisine, Patrick was ready for an answer. "OK, Mom," he said. "Fess up! How'd you get permission for us to eat in here?"

"OK, OK," Mrs. Tiller said. "A man who made a large contribution to the Mount Vernon Ladies' Association had asked permission to bring his children here for dinner. When he had to cancel suddenly, he asked me to enjoy the dinner with my own children and their guests."

"How nice of him," Christina said.

"Yes," Mrs. Tiller said. "Not many people can say they've eaten in George Washington's grand dining room—at least no one from the 21st century."

"Is this the largest room in the house?" Christina asked.

"It is," Mrs. Tiller replied. "It was also the last addition Washington made to Mount Vernon. It took more than 10 years to complete, and it was much more than a dining room. As the most formal room in the house, many important things happened here. It was in this very room that Washington learned he'd been elected the first president of the United States. And it was here that Washington's body lay for three days before his burial."

"Washington's b-b-body was in this r-r-room?" Grant asked, glancing around to make sure there were no other bodies lying around. KER-SPLASH! Grant's elbow hit his glass sending water splattering across the table and onto the floor.

Christina was mortified. "GRANT!" she yelled. "You spilled your drink on George Washington's rug!" She grabbed her napkin and mopped furiously.

"It's OK, Christina," Mrs. Tiller said. "I knew something like this was likely to happen. That's why you're drinking water and not red

Kool-Aid. And I've got plenty of plastic under this tablecloth and on the floor."

When she finished mopping up Grant's spill, Christina sat back down and noticed a familiar pain in her foot—the tooth! In all the excitement of the past hour, she had forgotten all about the tooth she'd found at Washington's tomb. She decided it was time to get one thing settled once and for all.

"Mrs. Tiller?" Christina asked. "We learned a lot about Mount Vernon today. Have you ever thought of creating a scavenger hunt to help kids learn about Mount Vernon?"

"No, I haven't," she answered. "But that's a great idea, Christina!"

Christina could tell from her expression that Mrs. Tiller had nothing to do with the clues they'd found. That left one big question to answer. Who did?

"Now," Mrs. Tiller said. "Are you kids ready for the rest of your surprise?"

"There's more?" Patrick asked.

"Yes!" Mrs. Tiller answered. "The large donor I told you about also had permission to spend the night here!"

"We're spending the night in George Washington's house?" Christina asked, incredulous.

"Alone?" Grant added.

Before Mrs. Tiller could say more, eerie music poured from an adjoining room. Christina thought it sounded something like a piano with a sore throat.

Grant looked at Christina, wide-eyed. Nellie and Patrick smiled.

"Bill's playing the harpsichord!" Nellie said with delight.

Inside the small room, a man was busy playing the large instrument that hugged the wall. It looked similar to a piano except it had two keyboards, one on top of the other. "Mrs. Tiller asked me to entertain you with some period music," Bill said as he played a cheerful tune on the harpsichord.

"This is my mom's assistant," Nellie explained. "He's one of the few people around who knows how to play the harpsichord."

"Why don't you tell them about this harpsichord," Bill suggested.

Nellie blushed. "This is my harpsichord," she said. "I mean it belonged to the person I was named for."

"Who was that?" Grant asked.

"Eleanor Parke Custis," Nellie replied. "Her nickname was Nellie, too. Mom was studying the Washington family when I was born, and she liked the name a lot."

"Who was she?" Christina asked.

"She was Martha Washington's granddaughter," Nellie answered. "The daughter of Martha's son, John Parke Custis. When John died, George and Martha took in his youngest children, Nellie and her brother George Washington Parke Custis. The Washingtons bought Nellie this harpsichord so she could learn to play."

Patrick gave a sweeping bow and asked Christina, "Would you care to dance, ma'am?" "Why certainly, sir," Christina replied with a big grin.

Grant wasn't interested. "Don't even ask!" he told Nellie.

Patrick whirled Christina around the small room while Grant, Nellie, and Mrs. Tiller clapped in rhythm. Christina took the opportunity to whisper in Patrick's ear, "We've got to get out of here!"

19
KEY TO WHERE OR WHAT?

The kids sat on top of their sleeping bags, still trying to believe they were really spending the night in George Washington's home. Mrs. Tiller had placed the sleeping bags in a circle near the bottom of the stair in the Passage. She said they were extremely fortunate to be spending the night, but sleeping in the beds was asking way too much. She had ordered them to "STAY PUT!" while she did a final check-in with the security guards at the gate.

The kids finally had a chance to talk.

"You confuse me," Patrick told Christina. "I thought you wanted to visit the mansion more than anything, and now, you tell me we've got to get out of here."

"Yes!" Christina said. "We've got to get out of here to find out where this tooth belongs and solve this mystery! Time is running out fast. Mimi and Papa will be here tomorrow."

Nellie agreed. "I don't want Mom to get into any trouble," she said. "And without Christina and Grant, we'll never get to the bottom of this."

"Well," Patrick said. "Mom ordered us to stay put, and that's what I'm planning to do."

"All I want to do is stay put," Grant said. "I'm stuffed as a turkey and bushed as a, as a, as a bush hog?" He flopped back on his sleeping bag and stretched. "Aaaaagh," he sighed and closed his eyes.

Christina sighed too. She had the once in a lifetime chance to sleep where George Washington had slept, and she was miserable. Suddenly, Grant sat up straight. "Is that key for emergencies?" he asked.

"What are you talking about," Christina asked, annoyed that Grant was interrupting her misery.

"It's in a glass case like those fire extinguishers that you break open for emergencies," Grant said.

Christina looked where Grant was pointing between two doorways. "It's just there for display," she said.

Then suddenly, the kids all stared at one another, mouths agape. They all realized at the same time that they were focused on the one thing the last clue had mentioned.

"KEY!" they shouted together.

"Could that be the one?" Christina asked, hopping up.

"That key is certainly priceless," Patrick said. "That was a key to the Bastille in France." Christina was glad to hear Patrick pronounce it correctly—*bas STEEL*.

"What's the Bastille?" Grant asked.

"It was a political prison in Paris," Patrick explained. "When citizens stormed the prison, it led to a revolution similar to the

American Revolution. The Marquis De Lafayette was a French commander who had earlier traveled to America to serve under George Washington. They were lifelong friends. He considered Washington a missionary of freedom. When the Bastille was demolished, he sent the key to Washington as a symbol of France's freedom."

"Let's take a look at it," Christina said. Patrick and Nellie watched in horror as Christina pushed a chair beneath the key display. She stood on the chair and examined the display.

"Mom would have a fit," Nellie whispered to Patrick.

"There's no way to open this case!" Christina said in frustration.

"You'll have to break it!" Grant said.

"Don't you dare!" Patrick shouted.

"Shhh!" Nellie said. "Mom's coming."

Christina continued to sweep her hands around the case and just in the nick of time climbed down, slid the chair back to its original position, and jumped onto her sleeping bag.

"Everything OK in here?" Mrs. Tiller asked when she returned. "At least it looks like everything's still in one piece. I told the guards we'd be going to the public restroom and then turning in for the night. You know, George and Martha didn't have the luxury of indoor plumbing. They had a Necessary House."

"Yeah," said Grant, squirming on his sleeping bag. "VERY necessary."

Mrs. Tiller laughed and motioned for the children to follow her.

After their visit to the public restrooms, as Christina was walking back toward the mansion, she glanced at the upper window and saw it again—the same shadowy figure she'd seen the night before was moving past the window.

When the kids returned to their sleeping bags, Mrs. Tiller snuffed the candles and soon everyone was asleep. Everyone except Christina. She could only toss, and turn, and listen. Mount Vernon popped and creaked occasionally like all old houses. But then Christina heard something much different. It was definitely the sound of footsteps. She could stand it no longer.

Christina crept around the sleeping bag circle and woke her cohorts. She spotted the flashlight Mrs. Tiller had left for them. Moonlight flooded in the windows, but she thought she'd better grab the flashlight anyway. Putting her finger to her lips, she motioned the others to follow her. She led them to George Washington's study, which Patrick had shown her earlier. Inside, she closed the door and turned on the flashlight. "There's something I need to show you," Christina told them. She opened her hand to reveal a long metal key.

"Did you break the case?" Grant asked.

"This key was on top of the key case," Christina said. "I didn't break anything. Now, we have to find what this key opens. And, we need to do it fast. I think there's someone upstairs."

20
CLUE CLOSEUP

Christina shined the flashlight around the study in search of any kind of case that had a lock. She noticed a small, wooden chest resting on a chair side table. But the key was much too large, and the case was already unlocked and empty.

"What about that desk?" Grant asked and yawned. A small desk crouched in front of a window. Christina tiptoed to it and pushed the key into the lock. This lock was larger than the key.

CREAK! CREAK!

Christina switched off the flashlight quickly. "Did you hear that?" she asked.

The kids froze until several minutes passed with no more sounds. Moonlight was shining so brightly into the study that the flashlight was no longer needed, and Christina clicked it off.

Grant stared at a painting. "He gives me the willies," Grant said. "I feel like he's watching us."

"That's Lawrence Washington," Patrick said. "George's half-brother. He's harmless." Christina looked around the room once more. "I guess there's nothing else in here that would open with a key," she said. "Maybe we should move to another room."

"Where's the tooth?" Grant asked. "The one you found at the tomb."

"Still in my shoe," Christina answered. "Why?"

"Maybe you should take a close look at it," Grant said. "It could give us a clue of where to look next."

Christina shrugged. She didn't see how looking at the tooth could help, but she didn't have any better ideas. She pulled off her shoe and felt inside. "Oh no!" she cried. "It's not there. I must have lost it!"

"Maybe you should have put it under my wig," Grant suggested.

Christina sat down to put her shoe back on when she snickered. "Found it!" she said. "It was stuck between my toes."

Grant turned the flashlight back on and shined it on the tooth. Like the other one they'd found, it had a small screw in the bottom.

"I wish we had a magnifying glass," Grant said. "There might be something we're missing."

"Would a telescope work?" Nellie asked. "George's brass telescope that he used to watch boats on the river is right here on this table."

"It's worth a try," Christina said. "Grant, you hold the tooth, and I'll look through the telescope. Nellie, you hold the flashlight on the tooth."

"You always take the fun jobs," Grant complained.

Christina swung the brass telescope around and aimed it at the tooth. "This works great!" she said. "It's like looking through a microscope."

"What do you see?" Grant asked impatiently.

All Christina said was, "Interesting, verrry interesting."

"Let me look!" Patrick said.

Before Christina could let him have a turn, they heard the CREAK, CREAK sound again. She motioned for Nellie to kill the flashlight. Once more they froze in position like Freeze Tag, held their breath, and waited, trying not to move or sneeze.

After several miserable minutes, Christina whispered. "Where did George Washington sleep?"

"In a bed," Nellie said.

Christina was glad it was too dark for Nellie to see her roll her eyes. "I mean which room did he sleep in?"

"The master bedroom on the second floor," Patrick said.

"Drats!" Christina exclaimed. "We'd probably wake your mom if we go back to the Passage and climb the stairs."

"Why do you want to go there?" Grant asked.

"Where do old people usually put their dentures?" Christina asked.

"Our grandpa puts his in a little plastic case on the nightstand by the bed," Nellie said.

"Exactly!" Christina said. "In George Washington's day they didn't have plastic, but maybe he kept a little wooden case by his bed for his dentures—a little wooden case he opened with a key!"

"Have you forgotten what you said about thinking someone might be upstairs?" Grant reminded his sister.

"I haven't forgotten," Christina said. "But we don't know for sure. What we do know for sure is that we're never gonna solve this mystery by standing here in the dark doing nothing!"

"I've got an idea," Patrick said. "Follow me!"

21
STAIRWAY OR NO WAY!

Patrick led them to another set of stairs.

"I didn't know there was another set of stairs!" Christina exclaimed.

"Washington didn't like to be disturbed when he was in his study," Patrick said. "It's where he wrote letters and managed Mount Vernon and helped plan a new nation. This way, he could get up in the morning and go straight to his study without waking anyone else."

Patrick led them into a large, but simple, bedroom. A bed with a canopy took up the space between two windows. It was hard to make out much else.

"Give me the flashlight," Christina whispered to Nellie.

She cautiously turned on the light, fearing they might see *who* or *what* had been making the creaky footsteps. She swept the light around the room and even under the bed and to her relief saw nothing.

Grant chuckled.

"What's so funny?" Christina asked.

"You know how all those places always claim that 'George Washington slept here?'" Grant said. "Well, George Washington really did sleep here!" He moved beside the bed and stretched. "I think I'll try out George's bed for myself."

"Ah, Graaant," Patrick said. "Did I also tell you that George died in this room?"

Grant quickly backed away from the bed. "Suddenly, I'm not feeling sleepy anymore," he said.

Christina carefully surveyed the room. There was a small writing desk that Martha Washington had probably used to write her letters, and more family portraits. On one side of the bed sat a small, round table and a single candlestick. Nothing looked promising until Christina's light fell upon a dressing table with a wooden case on top! She rushed to the case and to her amazement, the key fit the lock!

The others peered over her shoulder as it opened with a loud CREAK!

Christina wondered, was that the sound we heard before? She shined the light inside and was amazed to see a set of teeth smiling back at her! She gingerly lifted the dentures out of the box. Two of the teeth were missing. Christina fished the tooth out of her shoe and slipped it effortlessly into one of the sockets. "Perfect fit," she said.

"Mystery solved," Nellie said.

"Not quite," Christina said. "We may have found the *what*, but we still haven't found the *why* or the *who*. Besides, there's something very strange about these teeth."

"What's so strange about them?" Grant asked.

Christina fingered the eagle around her neck and answered. "They're made out of wood!" she said. "I suspected the tooth was wood when I saw it through the telescope." She handed the dentures to Grant. "Feel how light they are," she said. "Dentures made out of bone and human teeth like the ones we saw in the museum would be heavier than this."

"But I thought Washington's wooden teeth were a myth," Grant said, confused.

Once again, a loud CREAK! CREAK! startled the kids.

"It's above our heads again," Christina said. "What room would that be, Patrick?"

"Martha Washington's room," he answered. "Third floor."

"I thought this was Martha and George's room," Christina said.

Patrick replied, "After George died, Martha refused to stay in this room. She moved to the small bedroom on the third floor."

CREAK! CREAK!

"We've got to check it out," Christina said.

"If George Washington was brave enough to take on the British army, then I can be brave enough to go upstairs!" Grant said. "Good thing I still have my hatchet," he said, patting his side.

The kids climbed the stairs to Martha's room. The door was closed. Christina turned the knob, and they tiptoed, close together like a human train, through the door.

The room was much smaller than the master bedroom. When Christina saw the small dormer window, she realized it was the same third floor window where she'd seen the shadowy figure.

Just as the thought crossed her mind, a floorboard squeaked and the door closed with a SLAM!

Christina dashed to the door and opened it just in time to see someone climbing the ladder outside the room that led into the mansion's round cupola. She shined the flashlight into the cupola. A man with whiskers on his chin shielded his eyes from the light. "Come on down, Frank," she said.

"Frank?" Grant asked, confused.

"Hi, kids," Frank said sheepishly. "I was just doing a quick check of the grounds before I turned in for the night."

"Boy, I'm sure glad you're here," Grant said. "Look what we've found! George Washington's wooden teeth!"

"I think Frank already knows about the wooden teeth, don't you, Frank?" Christina asked.

Frank's kindly expression turned mean. "OK, give me the teeth now!" he said. "Hand them to me, and no one will get hurt."

The staircase below them suddenly rumbled like thunder with the sound of charging feet. "No one's getting hurt!" a deep voice said. Christina turned to see three security guards, and standing behind them, a disgusted Mrs. Tiller.

"How'd you know we were here?" Christina asked a guard.

"We saw strange lights moving around the mansion," one guard answered.

"Our flashlight," Christina said.

"Edward, what are you doing here?" Mrs. Tiller asked. "You know this will mean jail time for you!"

"Who's Edward?" Christina asked.

"Yeah," Grant said. "I'm confused. This is Frank, and he guards the edges of Mount Vernon dressed as a Revolutionary War soldier."

"No," Mrs. Tiller corrected. "This is Edward Barnes. He worked as a carpenter here at Mount Vernon until he was caught trying to sneak artifacts off the grounds. I had to fire him shortly after I started here. I didn't press charges but told him I better never catch him on the property again."

"Frank wasn't *stealing* artifacts this time," Christina said, taking the wooden teeth from Grant. "I think he was *making* them."

"I made those teeth and hid them around the property before I was fired," Frank confessed. "A few sets of Washington's wooden teeth, found at Mount Vernon, would have brought me a fortune."

"You were disguising yourself as a re-enactor and using us to gather the teeth to bring them to you," Christina said. "That way, even if you were caught, you could claim that *we'd* smuggled the teeth out of Mount Vernon."

Edward just hung his head.

22
DON'T FORGET TO FLOSS

Grant was polishing off his fourth hoecake, this time calling it breakfast instead of a snack, when he and Christina saw Mimi and Papa biking around the circle in front of Mount Vernon.

"I've got so much to tell you!" Christina said as she tried to squeeze the stuffing out of her grandparents.

"Me too!" Grant mumbled through a mouthful, spewing hoecake crumbs as he spoke.

"I'm glad to know we were missed," Mimi said. "Hello, Patrick and Nellie. Did you keep these two out of trouble and teach them lots of history?"

Patrick and Nellie smiled. "Let's just say we found out what good mystery solvers they are," Patrick said.

"Yeah," Nellie agreed. "From now on we'll be able to tell tourists at Mount Vernon that Christina and Grant slept here!"

"Tell me what you learned while you were here," Papa said.

"Don't chop down cherry trees...always tell the truth...and never talk to strangers!" Grant said, straightening his George Washington wig. "Especially if they live in the woods."

"Those are good things to know," Mimi said, suspiciously pondering Grant's last comment. "What about you, Christina?"

Christina said, "First, George Washington was so much more than a picture in my history book. Second, if you're going to dress like a colonial girl, carry a purse to put things in. And third, never try to solve a mystery unless Mimi and Papa are close enough to bail you out!"

When Mimi looked startled, Grant added, "And the most important thing we learned is..." He gave his friends a big, toothy grin and they all cried:

"FLOSS! FLOSS! FLOSS!"

Well, that was fun!

Wow, glad we solved that mystery!

Where shall we go next?

EVERYWHERE!

The End

Now...go to
www.carolemarshmysteries.com
and...

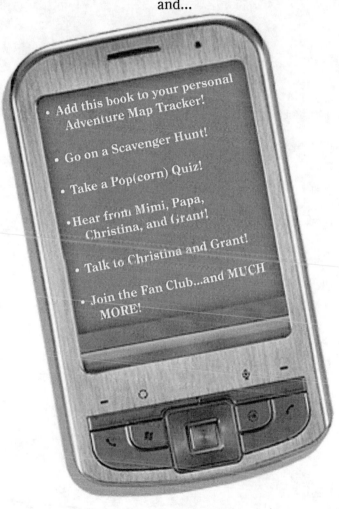

- Add this book to your personal Adventure Map Tracker!

- Go on a Scavenger Hunt!

- Take a Pop(corn) Quiz!

- Hear from Mimi, Papa, Christina, and Grant!

- Talk to Christina and Grant!

- Join the Fan Club...and MUCH MORE!

GLOSSARY

artifacts: objects of historic or cultural significance

blacksmith: a person who makes horseshoes and other iron tools

fife: a small flute-like musical instrument made with six to eight finger holes

ha-ha walls: low walls designed to keep in livestock without being seen from the house

pocketwatch: a small watch which was chained to trousers and kept in a pocket

sarcophagus: a stone coffin

survey: to measure and post a tract of land

treading house: a gristmill for grinding wheat

archaeology: the study of old things to find out about the past

whine: to beg or plead, or to sound as if begging

mischievous: fond of tricks

authentic: the real thing

ominous: a feeling or indication that something bad might happen soon

Enjoy this exciting excerpt from:

THE MYSTERY
IN
Hawaii

1
HOTEL HULA

Grant rubbed his blue eyes in wonder as they approached the entrance to the Royal Hawaiian Hotel, the oldest hotel on the Island of Oahu. His blond hair was more tousled than usual because of the long trip. He had stayed in many hotels with Mimi and Papa before, but this was different.

"Look, Christina," said Grant. "It looks like a big, creepy bottle of Pepto Bismol!"

"Maybe that's why they call it the Pink Palace," Christina replied. Tall and lean, with medium length dark hair and blue eyes, Christina towered over her younger brother.

Mimi and Papa were looking forward to staying in a hotel with such a rich history, but

Christina and Grant thought any hotel built in 1927 was just OLD!

Papa, looking handsome as always in his cowboy hat and boots, sauntered up to the registration desk.

"Name on the reservation, sir?" the desk clerk inquired.

"Papa, cowboy pilot of the *Mystery Girl*!" he replied proudly.

"Uh, actually, the reservation is under Carole Marsh," Mimi said. She wore a brand new red suit with matching shoes that she bought just for this special vacation.

"Whatever the beautiful blond lady says," Papa said. "I just want to get this vacation started. By the way, why in the world did you have to bring that extra suitcase along, Mimi? You know I hate to get bogged down with luggage overload."

"Take it easy, Papa," Mimi said with a sly smile. "We need to have something to carry our souvenirs back in, right?"

"Well, yeah, but as heavy as that bag is already, the only souvenir you can get is a lei!"

Papa said.

"Come on, Christina, let's go check out the beach!" yelled Grant.

Mimi spun around and with a stern look, said, "PLEASE USE YOUR INDOOR VOICE, Grant!" The gruff-looking man at the front desk nodded in agreement with a sneer.

"Uh, OK, how about I take my indoor voice outdoors?" Grant asked. "Come on, Christina," he said again, and made a beeline for the door.

As Christina and Grant stopped to look at the kids' pool, a friendly young girl spoke to them. "Did you know," she said, "that Hawaiian King Kamehameha once used this area as his personal playground in the late 1700s, before the hotel was built?"

Christina and Grant turned around to see a Hawaiian girl with beautiful, long dark hair and tanned skin.

"Yeah, and did you know that Shirley Temple was born here?" added a young boy standing beside her.

"No, Kalino, the Shirley Temple cocktail

was invented here!" the girl replied, rolling her eyes. "Hi, my name is Haumea and this is my little brother Kalino. What are your names?"

"I'm Christina and this is MY little brother Grant," Christina said. "Pleased to meet you!"

"Are you on vacation, too?" asked Grant.

"No, we live here," said Kalino. "Maybe we could show you around the island. How long will you be here?"

"Not very long," said Christina. "We're leaving tomorrow evening for Maui."

"The island of Maui is beautiful," Haumea said with a smile. "Kalino and I have visited all six of the Hawaiian islands several times with our parents. We can tell you the coolest things to see."

"Hey, I have an idea. Why don't I ask Mimi and Papa if you could come with us?" said Christina.

"I'll ask our parents and let you know. Thanks!" said Haumea. "By the way, watch out for the man at the front desk at your hotel.

Every kid I've talked to who has stayed here has said..." Haumea stopped talking to look at her watch. "Whoops," she said, "come on Kalino, it's later than I thought. Sorry, Christina, but we have to go. I promised my dad we would be back 20 minutes ago. Talk to you later!"

Something occurred to Christina a moment later. "Wait, what about the man at the hotel?" she yelled. The kids were already out of earshot.

So Christina was left wondering what in the world they had to "watch out for."

2
LUAU LADIES

Without getting Papa's or Grant's opinion, Christina and Mimi decided the first order of business was to attend a real Hawaiian luau. The beach was decorated with flaming Tiki torches which flickered red and gold, making the ocean waves sparkle. Each luau table was piled high with purple and yellow hibiscus flowers, wooden dishes, and elaborate centerpieces made from bamboo.

"Look, there are men in girly skirts and necklaces!" Grant said, giggling.

"Those aren't girls' skirts, silly," said Christina. "They're hula skirts, which are part of the costume used to perform traditional Hawaiian dance to music. The flower necklaces are called leis. They are made by sewing tropical flowers to a delicate type of rope."

Grant was about to speak, when all of a sudden he turned and came eye to eye with an enormous dead pig stretched out on a wooden platter. A fat, red apple was stuffed in its mouth, with a pink and purple lei around its neck.

"Why would they try to feed that poor dead pig?" Grant asked.

"They're not feeding him, Grant—he's our dinner!" Papa said. "They cook him in the pit over there for several hours until the meat is as tender as can be. I can't wait to dig in!"

"I still don't understand why they didn't feed him BEFORE he died!" Grant argued.

While Mimi and Papa learned to hula dance, Christina and Grant explored the beach. The night air was filled with the smell of bougainvillea—and smoked pig.

As they walked barefoot in the surf, Christina spied the shadow of someone hiding behind a couple of towering palm trees. All of a sudden, the figure jumped out from behind the trees. Without hesitation, she yelled, "RUN!" and Grant quickly followed. Whoever was hiding was now running after them. Christina looked behind as she ran and noticed a second figure had joined the chase.

"Faster!" she pleaded.

They turned away from the beach and ran toward another hotel, hoping to evade their followers. Suddenly they heard someone scream, "Christina, stop!" When Christina turned to look, she was immediately relieved. "You scared us half to death, Haumea!" Grant said, as he tried to catch his breath.

"You guys ran so fast we couldn't catch up to let you know it was just me and Kalino," Haumea said. She slung her arm around Christina's shoulder. "Hey," she said, "I know a little shop about two minutes from here that sells the sweetest pineapple juice on the island. You two could probably use a cold drink after that run!"

"We're in!" Christina said, still gasping for breath.

As the kids headed on down the beach, they failed to notice more palms, more shadows, and more suspicious eyes watching them.